SUPERHERO SCHOOL

Aaron Reynolds
illustrated by **Andy Rash**

BLOOMSBURY

NEW YORK BERLIN LONDON

Leonard was the only kid on his Little League team who could hit a baseball into orbit.

He was the only kid in his class who had clobbered a giant lava monster.

He was the only kid on his block who had welded the Bay City Bridge back together using heat vision. So when his mom told him he was going to a special school, he saw it coming a trillion billion light-years away.

Leonard couldn't wait for Superhero School to start.

He was fired up to leap tall buildings in a single bound. He was super pumped up to bend steel beams with his bare hands. He was revved up and raring to go to stop speeding runaway trains.

Monday at Superhero School . . . Leonard met his new teacher, The Blue Tornado. But instead of learning how to leap tall buildings, Leonard's class wrestled the times tables.

"I'm sure I'll be too busy destroying alien death rays to ever worry about multiplication," suggested Leonard.

Mr. Tornado just chuckled. This was very troubling.

Tuesday at Superhero School . . . Leonard was fitted for his superhero uniform. It had a cape and everything. But instead of learning how to bend steel beams with bare hands, the class battled division.

Leonard tried to distract his teacher with an in-depth discussion about vanquishing evil robots, but Mr. Tornado still assigned **25** division problems for homework. This was very disappointing.

Wednesday at Superhero School . . . Leonard's class
inspected Mr. Tornado's Vortex-Mobile. It was fully loaded
with front-mounted shrink ray, submarine-transformation
capability, and a coat of invisibility wax—all the best options.
But instead of learning how to stop a speeding runaway
train, Leonard's class conquered fractions.

"I just *love* fractions," said Mr. Tornado. Mr. Tornado
was starting to *annoy* Leonard.

Thursday was the same. No lessons in throwing stray missiles into outer space. No field trips to freeze an erupting volcano using only arctic breath. No classes on overthrowing supervillains and mad scientists. Leonard was getting sick of Superhero School.

So when the ice zombies struck, Leonard never saw
them coming.

On Friday, when the class arrived at school, the signs of a frosty struggle were everywhere.

Icicles!

Snowballs!

Empty Slurpee cups!

And a note:

Dear Superhero students,
Have kidnapped the teachers. Taking over the world. School canceled.
Best wishes,
The Ice Zombies

The class sprang into action quicker than a swarm of evil ninja grasshoppers.

But Leonard and Sarah were the only kids who could fly. The class was pretty heavy, so they split in exactly $\frac{1}{2}$.

"I'll take the girls," Sarah barked. "I'm not touching the boys."

Sarah could sometimes get super bossy. But even among superheroes, cooties had to be considered. The class zoomed straight to the Arctic Circle in no time flat.

Arriving at the zombies' lair, Leonard's class discovered a huge frozen wall **15** feet thick. Thank goodness for heat vision! But Leonard's eyes could blast through only **5** feet of ice. Not nearly enough. Luckily Jack and Maggie had heat vision too.

"Fire up those eyeballs!" said Leonard.

"Wait!" said Jack. "I need to take off my new glasses."

With Jack's heatproof titanium glasses safely in their little plastic case, the three gave the icy wall their full focus.

With **3** times the heat—KER . . . MELT!—they blazed an entrance in no time.

On the other side of the wall, the ice zombies were fired up and ready to rumble.

"There are too many of them!" cried Jack. "Too many zombies!"

Leonard counted quickly. "There are only **20**. We can take 'em!"

"We just need superstrength," shouted Sarah. "Who's got it?"

Leonard, Sarah, Diego, Ritchie, and Kim all raised their hands . . . **5** superstrong students. No sweat.

Leonard quickly divided the zombies between them. "That's **4** apiece!" shouted Leonard. "ATTACK!" And that's when Ritchie Zelinsky got stung by a bee. Good old Ritchie. Superstrong . . . and super allergic. Leonard quickly recalculated.

"That's **5** apiece!" shouted Leonard. "ATTACK!"

While Ritchie took his allergy medication and breathed deep, cleansing breaths, the other **4** kicked the ice cubes out of **5** ice zombies each. A cheer went up across the zombie-infested wasteland. The teachers were saved! And they had suffered almost no freezer burn. Almost.

The class soared back to school, teachers in tow, just before the last bell rang. But instead of thanking them for saving his life from certain doom, Mr. Tornado just said, "Well done, class. A+ on the math quiz."

MATH QUIZ?

And then it hit Leonard like a giant mutant octopus.

Splitting the class in $\frac{1}{2}$? FRACTIONS!
Heat vision times **3**? MULTIPLICATION!
Ice zombies divided by **5** students?
DIVISION!
It was an evil trick. But Leonard went
home for the weekend, oddly supersatisfied.

After that, multiplication was less troubling. Division was less disappointing. Fractions were less annoying. And once in a while, Leonard's class got to leap tall buildings and bend steel beams. Leonard had to admit, Superhero School was pretty super after all.

Besides, Leonard could always stop speeding runaway trains . . .

. . . on Saturday.

To Reese,
my little math whiz,
who still has the power to melt
my heart with a single smile
—AARON REYNOLDS

To Jennifer,
my secret source of power,
my atomic superwoman,
my partner in crime
—ANDY RASH

Published by Bloomsbury U.S.A. Children's Books
175 Fifth Avenue, New York, New York 10010

Library of Congress Cataloging-in-Publication Data
Reynolds, Aaron.
Superhero School / by Aaron Reynolds. — 1st U.S. ed.
p.   cm.
Summary: When Leonard starts attending Superhero School he is disappointed
to find that all they learn is math, but when the ice zombies strike, Leonard
and his classmates put their newly acquired knowledge to good use.
ISBN-13: 978-1-59990-166-4 • ISBN-10: 1-59990-166-8 (hardcover)
ISBN-13: 978-1-59990-346-0 • ISBN-10: 1-59990-346-6 (reinforced)
[1. Superheroes—Fiction. 2. Schools—Fiction. 3. Mathematics—Fiction.] I. Title.
PZ7.R33213Su 2009   [E]—dc22   2008031374

The art is a digital collage of gouache and Sharpie®
Typeset in Garth Graphic and Bernhard Gothic
Book design by Donna Mark

First U.S. Edition 2009
Printed in China by C&C Offset Printing Co. Ltd., Shenzhen, Guangdong
6 8 10 9 7 5   (hardcover)
2 4 6 8 10 9 7 5 3   (reinforced)

All papers used by Bloomsbury U.S.A. are natural, recyclable products
made from wood grown in well-managed forests. The manufacturing processes
conform to the environmental regulations of the country of origin.